I Can Read About
Birds

Written by Ellen Schultz
Illustrated by Lisa Bonforte

Troll Associates

Library of Congress Cataloging-in-Publication Data
Schultz, Ellen (date)
     I can read about birds / by Ellen Schultz ; illustrated
by Lisa Bonforte.
      p. cm.
   ISBN 0-8167-3642-1 (lib. bdg.). — ISBN 0-8167-3643-X (pbk.)
   1. Birds—Juvenile literature. [1. Birds.] I. Bonforte,
Lisa, ill. II. Title.
QL676.2.S328   1996
598—dc20   95-5947

Millions of years ago, when gigantic dinosaurs roamed the land, there lived a strange creature called Archaeopteryx (Ar-kee-OP-ter-ix). This creature was an ancestor of today's birds.

How strange it looked. It was a little larger than a crow, and it had a lizard-like body covered with dark feathers. It had lots of sharp teeth and long, pointed claws.

crow

Archaeopteryx

How different it was from the graceful, brightly colored birds that inhabit the earth today.

great blue heron

7

Today, there are close to 9,000 different species, or kinds, of birds.

hummingbird

bald eagle

penguin

bluebird

Although the species are different, all birds have several important things in common. They are warm-blooded. They lay eggs. They have feathers. And they have backbones and wings.

9

golden eagle

Birds are warm-blooded animals. They are able to control their body temperature, regardless of the outside weather.
Their hearts beat very rapidly, using a great deal of energy. In order to maintain this energy, most birds must eat several times an hour. Some baby birds eat their own weight in food a day.

great blue heron

Different birds
eat different foods.

black-capped chickadee

Swallows and
chickadees
eat insects.

Kingfishers and
herons catch fish
with their long,
powerful beaks.

sparrow

Sparrows like seeds.

And vultures, hawks, and owls eat rats, squirrels, and other birds. Birds do not have teeth to chew and grind their food. So most birds must swallow little pebbles. The pebbles take the place of teeth. They grind the food into a soft pulp so that the food can be easily digested.

goshawk

A bird's skeleton is strong and streamlined, just like an airplane. And birds have light, yet rigid, backbones. Their lightweight bones make it easier for them to fly. Many of their bones are long, thin, and hollow. Some of them actually fill with air to help keep the bird aloft.

bird skeleton

How different from the Archaeopteryx, whose bones were solid and heavy.

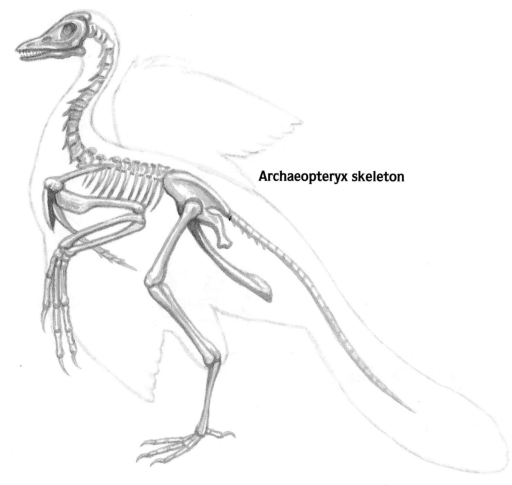

Archaeopteryx skeleton

The next time you see a bird, look closely at its wings. After takeoff, the wings move upward. The feathers spread apart to let the air through. Then the wings move downward.

The downstroke is most important. Because as the wings move down, they also push the bird through the air.

The feathers overlap so no air can pass through. In this way the bird is able to move through the air quickly. Then the wings move upward and the process begins again.

The bird uses its tail feathers for steering and stopping.

Some birds have developed long, graceful wings over millions of years. Their wings allow them to soar through the air for hours at a time.

The wandering albatross has the greatest wingspread of all, nearly 12 feet (3.7 meters) long.

wandering albatross

Not all birds can fly. The penguin and the ostrich have short, tiny wings that could never carry them off the ground. They prefer to stay on land or near the water.

When the ostrich is frightened, it does not stick its head in the sand. It either runs away or uses its strong legs to kick an enemy.

ostrich

penguin

The tiny hummingbird is the only bird that can fly backward. It is able to hover in the air like a helicopter. It flaps its wings so quickly that it is able to stay in one place. The wings move 60 to 70 times a second!

ruby-throated hummingbird

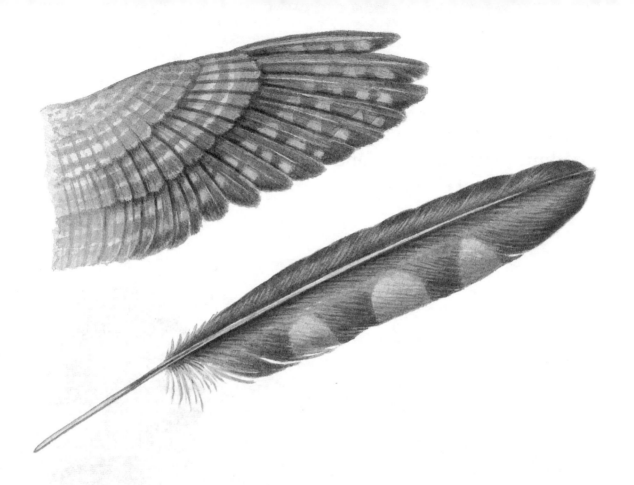

Have you ever looked closely at a feather? The largest of the feathers are the *primary* or *contour* feathers. These feathers are used in flight. Birds cannot fly without feathers.

Underneath the flight feathers are many soft feathers called *down*. These feathers keep the bird's body warm. Birds grow warm fluffy down as the winter season approaches.

Waterbirds, such as ducks and geese, usually have the thickest layer of waterproof down.

redhead duck

Canada geese

Sometimes, feathers break and fall out. When this happens, new feathers begin growing in to take their places. At least once each year, birds *molt*, or lose their old, worn-out feathers. But a bird always has enough feathers left to fly.

Some birds do not grow enough warm down to protect them from the cold winter. So as summer begins to turn into fall, certain species of birds make the journey to a warmer climate. This journey is called migration.

Birds will travel many different routes to a warm climate where there are plenty of plants and insects.

Some birds fly south during the daylight hours. Others fly after it is dark.

robins

bald eagle

Some birds fly south in large groups called *flocks*.
Others prefer to fly south all by themselves.

Their route is guided year after year by familiar things. Birds use mountains, oceans, cloud patterns, and stars to help guide them on their way. Once they arrive, they will spend three or four months in the warmer climate.

Canada geese

cardinal

Some birds, like the cardinal, stay at home all year round. They have learned how to adapt to the snow and where to find food in colder months.

As the days become longer and the weather turns warmer, a built-in time clock tells millions of birds that it is time to return to their northern homes. Birds just naturally know when to return home.

yellow warblers

Springtime is a time for courtship.
The males have colorful feathers, and they
fill the air with the sound of music.

song sparrow

But a bird does not sing only to attract a mate. Very often a bird's special melody is a warning to other birds to stay out of its territory. The little sparrow may sing its song twenty different ways.

owl

ostrich

catbird

    Birds also use their special language to warn other birds that an enemy is approaching. The timid ostrich makes a sound like a lion. The catbird meows just like a cat. And the owl hoots.

In the springtime, the loveliest songs are sung by the males to the females. As soon as a mate has been chosen, the couple gets down to the serious business of building a nest. Usually, the male selects the nesting site, while the female gathers the building materials. These may be grasses, twigs, hairs, pebbles, plants, mud . . . whatever can be found.

robins

cowbird

downy
woodpecker

owl

Woodpeckers make holes in dead tree trunks. Burrowing owls use tunnels below the ground. The lazy cowbird just lays its eggs in another bird's nest. And bald eagles build nests high in trees or on rocky ledges.

The bald eagle makes the largest nest in North America. The largest ever found measured 20 feet (6 meters) deep and almost 10 feet (3 meters) wide.

bald eagle

hummingbird

The hummingbird's nest is so small that it will fit inside a soda bottle cap or into an empty walnut shell.

Most birds lay from four to eight eggs a year. Different species have eggs that are different sizes and colors. The biggest egg of all is the ostrich egg. It is wide and round and weighs about 3 pounds (1.4 kilograms). The hummingbird lays the smallest eggs.

Some eggs are speckled. Others are white, blue, brown, green, red, or gray.

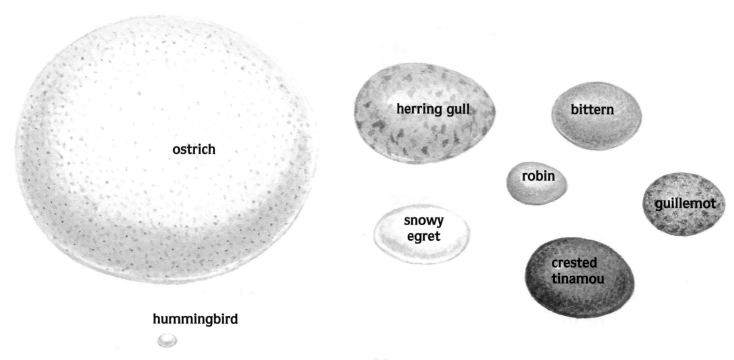

chicken

Inside the egg, the tiny baby gets nourishment from the yellow yolk and from the white albumen that surrounds it.

The eggs will not develop unless they are kept warm. The female is usually the one to sit on them. This is called *brooding*. The length of time before the eggs hatch depends on the type of bird. Hummingbird eggs hatch in ten days to two weeks. An ostrich egg takes as long as six weeks.

ostrich

chicken

When the young bird is ready to hatch,
it begins by bumping its egg tooth against the shell.
The egg tooth is a hard little tip on the end of the beak used to crack
open the shell. Little by little, the baby is able to open up the shell so
that it can wriggle out. In a short time the egg tooth will fall off.

Most newborn baby birds are covered with soft furry down. Their eyes are usually open. By the end of the day they are able to feed themselves, run around, or swim with their parents.

mallard

But some birds, such as woodpeckers, parrots, and hawks, are born blind and helpless. They must stay in the nest until they can open their eyes and move around. During this time, their parents feed and protect them.

green woodpecker

In a week or two, most young birds have grown full feathers and are ready to fly. When they hop over the edge of the nest, there is no turning back. They must either fly on their own the first time or fall to the ground. Many baby birds do amazingly well the first time.

The parents guide them until they are strong enough to be on their own. Then they must find their own food and defend themselves against all enemies, for they will never return to the nest.

Now they are ready for the world. Now a new life cycle will begin again.

song sparrows

It all happens in the wonderful world of birds.

robins